A CRYSTAL ANGEL

A MARSDEN ROMANCE 1.5

DAWN BROWER

This is a work of fiction. Names, characters, places, and incidents are products of the author's imagination or are used fictitiously and are not to be construed as real. Any resemblance to actual locales, organizations, or persons, living or dead, is entirely coincidental.

A Crystal Angel Copyright © 2015 Dawn Brower

Cover art by Victoria Miller

CONTENTS

Chapter One   1
Chapter Two   13
Chapter Three   25
Chapter Four   34
Chapter Five   46
About The Author   55
Also by Dawn Brower   57
Afterword   63
Acknowledgments   65

DAWN BROWER   *Excerpt: A Flawed Jewel*
               Chapter One   69

DAWN BROWER   *Excerpt: A Treasured Lily*
               Chapter 1   89

DAWN BROWER   *Excerpt: A Sanguine Gem*
               Chapter One   103

This book is for everyone who wants more of Pia and Thor. I hope you enjoy it as much as I did writing it. I want to acknowledge all the people who helped make me look good: Christina, Debbie, Amanda, and especially my editor, Jennifer. I can't say thanks enough.

December 1875

*A*n emerald green vase flew across the room, hit the wall, and shattered into thousands of tiny shards. Quick reflexes allowed Thor, Viscount Torrington, to shift his head just in time to avoid it nearly connecting with his skull instead of the wall behind him.

"Pia, you really need to calm—"

This time a bronzed horse, crafted in mid-gallop, flew at him as he dodged to the right of his desk. He needed to subdue his wife before she permanently injured him. At the very least he wanted to stop her from breaking any other pieces of furniture or knick-knacks lying about his study in her fit of rage. He didn't know what had brought on this impromptu temper tantrum, but he'd already had enough of it. The previous night's overindulgence hadn't left him feeling well. His stomach churned and his head ached something fierce. He'd been sitting at his desk the better part of the afternoon staring at the same business reports, unable to decipher the meaning of them.

"How dare you tell me to calm down. I know what you did, you bloody idiot." Pia stormed towards him, waving a rolled parchment within her tight grasp. She twirled it around in circles with each step closer to him, her face growing a deeper shade of red. "You have a lot of explaining to do. What made you think this bit of nonsense would ever be a good idea?"

Thor pinched the bridge of his nose as pain shot daggers through his skull. He'd been out playing cards with the Earl of Devon the night before, attempting to persuade him into doing a bit of business with him. The events of the night before were a bit sketchy in his throbbing head.

"I don't have a clue what you're talking about."

"Well, if you hadn't decided to get sloshed with the Earl of Devon last night maybe you'd recall agreeing to betroth your son to his only daughter."

"What? Of course I wouldn't."

Her eyebrows rose in derision, her pale blonde curls framing her red face. "Oh really? That's why the Earl sent over this document outlining it in fine details. He even signed it. His note says it has all of the items you discussed last night and he looks forward to doing business with you in the future. Just sign it and send it to his solicitors."

Some of it started to come back. Devon had mentioned something about tying their families together. His daughter, Gemma, was a couple of years younger than the twins, Lily and Liam. Though they never really had any opportunity to interact with each other, Thor wondered why Devon would think Liam and Gemma would make a good match.

"Let me see it."

Pia threw the paper on his desk and folded her arms across her chest. Her blue eyes glared at him as he opened up the document and read it. Thor scanned the contents and clenched his fists. Damn it, she was right. He was a bloody fool.

"You're right. It's a betrothal. In my defense, I don't recall agreeing to this."

"Well, you can just send Lord Devon an apology.

We do not choose who our children decide to marry."

How to explain it wasn't going to be as easy as she thought. He didn't want to betroth Liam to the earl's daughter, but it might already be too late.

"Now Pia..."

"Don't even start, Thor. You messed up and you're going to fix it. Unless you want this to be the birthday and Christmas present you give your son this year. The twins are going to be turning fourteen this Christmas. Liam just got home from Eton. Are you prepared to spoil the holiday with your fool-ishness?"

"I don't know if it's that easy." Apprehension filled him as he stared at his wife.

"Of course it is. Go over and tell him you're a drunken idiot and you made a mistake. Trust me, if you don't make this go away, I promise you'll regret it."

Thor ran his fingers through his hair and sighed in frustration. He didn't like it when Pia was angry with him. He had to repair this damage before his wife did some irreparable harm to an important appendage of his. No doubt it would be the most heinous of deeds.

"I assure you, I already do."

"Good. Don't bother touching me until you make sure the Earl of Devon understands you are not signing a betrothal contract. I don't want anything to do with a man who plans on forcing his son to marry someone he doesn't love. I love you, Thor, but I have to do what I think is best for our children."

"Pia—wait! Stop"

Pia spun on her heels, ignoring him, as she stormed out of the room. A few strands of her pale blonde hair had come loose and floated around her neck as she breezed out. Her feet stomped hard on the ground, echoing through his study in rhythm with the pounding in his head.

"Bloody hell, what a mess."

Thor stood up and walked out of his study. It looked like he would need to pay a call on the Earl of Devon. He had to clear up this mess if he ever wanted to bed his wife again.

LILLIANA BREEZED INTO THE ROOM, smugness oozing out of her. She couldn't wait to tease her brother with a bit of the information she just stumbled into.

"You are not going to believe what I just heard our parents arguing about."

Liam looked up from the chessboard, pale blond hair framing his face. "I don't really care. I'm trying to concentrate."

"On what?" Lily asked.

"Beating His Grace here in a game of chess."

"Don't let him fool you. He doesn't stand a chance. He has yet to beat me." Noah St. John, the Duke of Huntly and Liam's best friend, laughed as he watched him study the board.

"You should care, it was all about you after all."

Liam stopped staring at the chessboard and looked up at Lily. "I didn't do anything at school, I swear."

"Got a bit of a guilty conscience, do you?" Lily couldn't help asking him as a feeling of mischief rooted through her.

Noah's brown eyes widened with horror. "You don't think they heard about the incident, do you?"

"Of course not. No one knows it was us. They wouldn't have had time to send any notice to my parents." Liam paused and tilted his head in consideration. "Of course, anything is possible. At least you don't have parents they would send any notice to. Your guardian can barely be bothered to check up on you."

"I wouldn't call it luck."

Noah's face lost all color at the mention of his parents, his mouth forming a straight, grim line. They died the year before in a horrific carriage accident, leaving him alone in the world. He had no family to speak of and a solicitor for a guardian. Once he reached majority he would take over control of his lands and title, but for the moment he needed someone to do it for him. It was the reason he came home with Liam from Eton on every break since his parents died.

"You shouldn't pick on your friend, Liam."

Lily didn't have any friends of her own and sometimes found herself a bit jealous of Liam's relationship with Noah. She didn't have the luxury of going away to school, and many of the girls her age didn't like her. She longed for the day she would have a friend who understood her. Of course, she was also realistic and didn't expect it to happen.

"I have to ask"—Lily's curious nature took over —"what did you two do?"

"Nothing," both boys chimed in at once.

"I don't believe you."

"We can't tell you."

Noah nodded his head in agreement. "It would break the oath we took."

Lily stared at the boys, studying each of their

faces. Both of them had carefully schooled features, not an ounce of emotion showing, equally determined not to reveal their secret. She decided it didn't matter what they did. Well to be more apt, it didn't matter in that moment. She'd still get the details out of them, but her other news would send Liam into fits.

"All right. I suppose I can let it go for now."

"Good, 'cause we didn't plan on telling you." Liam turned back to concentrate on the chessboard.

"Why'd you give in so easy?" Noah asked.

"Don't see the point. Besides I think we need to discuss what I overheard."

"If it isn't about school, I don't care."

"You should, Liam. I told you it would impact your life."

"Well, what is it then?"

"Father agreed on a betrothal contract."

"Failing to understand how this might concern me." Liam waved his hand dismissively and turned back to his game. "Who is he going to marry you off to?"

"Not me you, fool. The Earl of Devon sent one over for him to sign. He's going to marry you off to his daughter, Lady Gemma Kemsley."

Liam's face turned stark white and he swayed in

his chair. He turned to look at Lily as the shock settled in. His blue eyes glazed over as the astonishment of her words became clear. "Pardon me, what did you say?"

"You're betrothed, as in when you both come of age, you're getting married. Congratulations, brother of mine."

"No. Why would he do that?"

"I don't know. Have to say I'm glad it's you and not me. If I marry I plan on doing it for love. I'm not making my marriage some kind of business contract."

Noah stood up and placed his hand on Liam's shoulder. "I'm sorry. What can I do?"

"Turn back time and make my father see how unwise this is."

"I would if I could. Maybe if you go talk to him..."

"Won't make a difference," Lily interrupted him. "If mother can't change his mind, no one can."

"I'm doomed." Liam crumpled in his chair, his head slumping over into his arms, resting on the table.

Lily rolled her eyes. "Oh, don't be so melodramatic. Maybe this Gemma girl is lovely."

"I don't care if she's the most beautiful docile chit

in all of England. I'm going to hate her just on principle."

Lily shook her head. "How mean and rude of you. At least give her a chance. If you're going to marry her, you do realize you have to spend the rest of your life with her? It wouldn't be good to get off to such a horrible start."

"What do you care? You aren't the one he's making marry someone you've never met." Liam turned to glare at his sister.

Lily stared at the mulish expression on her brother's face and a wave of sympathy rolled through her. He was her only real friend and she wanted to help him if she could. She might have teased him, but she didn't want him to have an unhappy life. There had to be some way to undo what their father had done.

"Well, maybe we'll just have to come up with a plan to persuade him against it."

"You just said it was a futile endeavor!" Liam exclaimed.

"Don't give your sister a hard time for wanting to help you." Noah turned toward Lily and gave her his full attention. "What do you have in mind?"

"We could run away."

"What good would that do?" Liam scoffed at her idea.

"It would make him realize how dead set you are against it. If we leave, it would show him we would rather live alone than deal with such disrespect for our wishes."

"Where would we go?" Liam asked.

"We could go to Huntly. The servants would welcome someone to take care of."

Liam looked at Noah and appeared to think about his suggestion. He shrugged as a look of defeat crossed his features. "I suppose it's as good a plan as any. Maybe this can all be resolved before Christmas. If not, I don't want to be here anyway."

"Go pack a small bag that you can carry. We can walk over to my townhouse and hitch a carriage to take us all the way to Huntly."

"Why don't we just stay there?" Lily asked.

Liam shook his head and replied, "It'd be the first place they looked. It's too close. We need to get their attention. Going to Huntly will slow them down a bit. I think we should leave a note saying we took one of the Marsden ships to America."

"Good idea. Liam, you write the note and I'll go pack a quick bag for the both of us. Noah, you get whatever you need from your room and let's meet out front in thirty minutes."

Both boys nodded at Lily and they took off to complete their tasks. Lily went upstairs and packed a small reticule for her and one for Liam. She grabbed each bag and poked her head out her bedroom door. No one was around, so she quietly sneaked out to the front of the house to await the two boys. Soon they would be at Huntly and hopefully their father, Viscount Torrington, would realize the error of his ways.

CHAPTER TWO

*P*ia walked into the sitting room and found an abandoned chessboard. Earlier when she checked on them, Liam and Noah had been deeply engrossed in the match. Now the room stood empty and the game unfinished.

"I wonder where the boys are?"

"Excuse me, ma'am."

Pia turned to see Tully directly behind her. "What is it?"

"I wondered if you realized the children all went out earlier."

"No, I didn't. Do you know where they were going?"

"No ma'am, but they each had a reticule."

What were her wayward children up to now?

"Why didn't you stop them?"

"I tried, ma'am. I saw them from the upper window. By the time I got it open they were long gone."

Tully could be so vexing. She didn't know why she put up with her childhood maid. She looked back at the chess set and saw a scrap of parchment sitting on one of the chairs. She picked it up and read Liam's note.

"Those bloody fools. They get this nonsense from their father. I'm going to wring their necks when I get hold of them."

Of course, she didn't mean to actually do any real harm to the twins, but the fright of their running away ran rapid through her head. She hoped nothing serious happened to them while they were out alone in the cold.

"What did the children do now?" Thor's voice bellowed from the open doorway.

"They ran away. It's your fault too."

"How's it my fault?"

"Your stupid contract with the Earl of Devon caused this." Pia flung the note at him. It fluttered in the air and floated to the ground at Thor's feet. He picked it up and scanned the contents.

"Bloody hell."

"Exactly. Now go get those children before someone kills them."

Thor pinched the bridge of his nose and shook his head. "Pia, I'm getting tired of your constant harping. You need to take a step back and think about what you're saying."

"Don't patronize me. I have every right to be worried about our children's welfare."

"I'm not disputing that, but you need to calm down—and before you start off into another temper tantrum, you'll see I'm right. If we're going to find our children we need to have clear heads. Acting out in anger isn't going to achieve anything good."

Pia glared at him and attempted to rein in her anger, as she could see his point. No matter how annoyed she was with Thor, attacking him wouldn't get any desirable results. She needed to focus on what was important—finding the twins and Noah.

"All right, I can see your point, but I'm still mad at you."

His lips tilted into a cocky grin and he winked at her. "Duly noted. Now let's go find the children. It says they are boarding a ship to America."

"Probably Lily's idea. She always asks to go back to Charleston."

"We don't have any ships going to America until

15

after the New Year. I should be able to catch them at the docks," Thor explained.

Pia decided she didn't trust Thor to handle the children. They probably thought they could outmaneuver them and escape. It might be Christmas, and their birthdays, but they were still going to be punished for their behavior. They were not even fourteen yet and shouldn't be out on their own.

"Fine, I'll go with you."

"It's unnecessary, Pia. I can take care of this."

"Forgive me if I don't have faith in your abilities. You've ruined Christmas with your blundering already."

Thor sighed. "Are you going to continue to harp on me about this for the rest of the holiday?"

"Yes. You haven't made up for your mistake yet, but I'm willing to let it go for the moment. Did you talk to Devon?"

"I did. He said he wished I'd reconsider, but understood why I wouldn't sign the contract. He urged me to keep it in case I changed my mind."

"I hope you explained it wasn't likely."

"I did, but I kept the contract to make him happy. I still want to do business with him sometime in the future. I put it in one of the locked drawers."

"Fine. As long as you don't plan on signing it, I'm all right with that. Let's go get the twins and Noah."

Pia walked out of the sitting room and grabbed her pelisse. She donned it and turned toward her husband. "Well, what are you waiting for?"

Thor just shook his head and led her out the front door. The carriage still sat out front from when Thor had gone to see the Earl. The footman and driver looked surprised to see them out so soon.

"We need to go to the waterfront. Make it fast," Thor explained to the driver as he turned to help Pia inside. She shoved his hand away, lifted her skirts and stepped into the carriage unassisted. Thor pursed his lips in frustration and followed her.

The carriage ride was swift and bumpy as they traveled to the dockyard. Pia glared at Thor the entire journey, obviously still blaming him for the fiasco they were now dealing with. Once they arrived at the docks, Thor jumped out and helped Pia out of the carriage, and they began to search for signs of the three children.

"I don't think they are here."

"We need to go farther down the wharf to make sure," Thor replied. "The docks are extensive and they could be hiding behind something."

They continued down the pier, Pia trailing after

Thor, holding her skirts so they didn't skim the dirty waterfront. Night had fallen, and the only light they had to guide their path was the moonlight streaming down from above, making it difficult for them to see anything clearly. They searched the entire area surrounding them without any luck locating the children.

"I don't see them," Thor exclaimed.

"Do you see them anywhere?" Pia asked at the same time Thor spoke.

"No, I don't see them. I'm beginning to think they're not here," Thor repeated his earlier conjecture.

Pia sighed as irritation set in; Thor could be so difficult.

"So, you're ready to give up on finding them. Leave them out here alone and cold."

"Of course not. I just think this was a diversion of theirs. They probably went someplace else. Liam knows more about Marsden Shipping than you realize."

"Have you started dragging him to business meetings already? I told you not to overwhelm him with all the inner workings of your many projects. He's too young to worry about these things."

Thor stopped in his tracks and pinned Pia with a

furious glare. She sucked in a breath as rage flared across his features. She'd gone too far and now he'd finally snapped under her constant rants. "Enough, Pia, I'm not going to listen to you shriek the rest of the night. As far as Liam goes, I don't want him unprepared. It's why I was taken advantage of."

Pia knew Thor hated any reminders of her grandpère; the Comte had tried to murder him to gain control of their shared company. He failed, but it hadn't ended there. Thor kidnapped Pia to get revenge on him. It didn't turn out as planned; it had gone a whole lot better. If he hadn't wanted revenge, they would never have found each other. They both agreed everything ended the way it was supposed to. Of course, agreeing they belonged together didn't mean they always agreed on how to handle their children.

Pia forced herself to calm down and reply to him in an even, neutral voice. "Liam isn't you. He doesn't have a business partner; he only has you. Give him time to grow up." This wasn't a new argument. Pia often berated her husband for trying to get Liam working at Marsden Shipping; hollering at him wouldn't make a lick of difference.

Thor scowled at her and explained, "I haven't been. It doesn't mean the lad isn't curious. He finds himself in my study all on his own. I'm not going to turn him away just because you think he's too young to learn it."

"Hmmph. Fine. I still think he's too young, but if he comes in on his own, I see your point."

She didn't see any reason to argue any further about it. Thor believed he needed to start learning and soon. It was his belief if he didn't start soon he would be at a loss when it was time for him to take over. Pia just wanted him to enjoy his childhood for as long as possible before taking on so much responsibility. When he gained his majority he could take his rightful place at Marsden Shipping and learn all he needed to know. Pia didn't think he would ever have a disadvantage, especially with Thor at his side each step of the way.

"Do you think someone may have kidnapped them?"

"What? No, of course not. No one would dare."

"You seem awfully certain of that," Pia whispered.

"They know what I used to be and an ex-pirate isn't someone to mess with. No one would hurt our children for fear of what I might do to him. No, the kids just ran away to prove a point."

"Which is your fault."

"Don't start again, Pia. I'm not going to make

Liam marry someone. When he gets married, it will be his choice."

"Still, we wouldn't be out in this frigid weather if you hadn't gotten inebriated with your crony the earl last night."

Pia couldn't stop herself from berating him, her worry for the children clouding her judgment. She wanted to find them as soon as possible and Thor made a good target for her anxiety. His face was etched with worry barely visible in the moonlight. She bit her lip and tried to prevent another irate outburst from spilling out of her mouth.

"Pia, do you really want to sit out here and argue or do you want to look someplace else?"

She inhaled and exhaled, her breath visible in the darkness. "Where do you suggest we look?"

"Noah's townhouse. They're not stupid and would know they needed someplace warm to stay. Since Noah is our guest, naturally they would go to his home."

"Do you really think they went there?"

She studied him, her pale blonde hair escaping the tight chignon and framing her face. He reached over and cupped her face in the palm of his hand. She stared up into his eyes finding her own love reflected back at her. No matter what, she knew she could depend on him. Yes, he had made a mistake, but he was willing to rectify it. He had done as she asked and retracted the betrothal contract with the Earl of Devon. He would have done it regardless because it was the right thing to do. Pia realized how awful she had been acting toward him and wished she hadn't acted like a shrew. No one else, besides her, loved the twins more. She knew if he thought the children had gone to Noah's townhouse, then they had. She needed to trust him as her instincts screamed at her to do.

"Yes, I do."

"All right. I will trust your judgment. Let's go look."

Thor led her to the carriage and helped her back inside. Once she was snuggled under one of the carriage blankets, Thor told the driver to take them to the Duke of Huntly's townhouse. The carriage rattled along the uneven road and the clip-clop of horses' hooves lulled them with their even rhythm. After what seemed like hours, the carriage came to a stop. Thor looked out the carriage window. Pia could see an ornate townhouse from the open slot in the carriage. Thor opened the door and hopped out, turning to assist Pia.

"I thought we would never get here," she exclaimed.

They raced up to the front door and knocked. After an eternity, or what seemed like one, the door finally cracked open. A wrinkled man in his bedclothes answered the door. His eyes narrowed at them, and with a gruff voice he asked, "What can I do for you?"

"Pardon the late hour, but has the young Duke of Huntly been by with our children, Lily and Liam?" Thor asked.

"His Grace was here briefly about two hours past. He ordered a carriage round to take him to the country estate. I didn't see any other children with him."

"Are you sure?" Pia bit her lip and wrung her hands together as worry nestled deep inside.

"I'm fairly certain I didn't see anyone else. His Grace came inside all alone. He awaited the carriage and after it arrived I only saw him enter it. I can't say if he picked anyone else up along the way."

"Well, there's nothing else we can do. Thank you for your time." Thor nodded at the older man and walked away from the door.

"What do you mean there isn't anything else we can do? We have to keep looking for our children."

"Of course we do, but they're not here."

"Clearly, but where are they?"

"That's easy enough; they are at the country estate of the Duke of Huntly."

"But the old man said he didn't see them." Pia's face scrunched up in puzzlement.

Thor leaned down and placed a quick kiss on her lips. "We have very intelligent children, Pia. They waited down the road and hopped in when no one else was paying attention. They tried to make it look like young Noah went home alone."

Pia bit her lip as she considered his words. She nodded her head, agreeing with his assessment. "So we're going to Huntly Manor?"

"Yes, we are. Get ready for a bit of a journey, love."

They both huddled into the carriage and sat back for the long ride to the country. The kids had a two-hour head start on them and would hopefully be safe inside by the time they arrived. There would be hell to pay once they caught up with their wayward children.

CHAPTER THREE

The carriage traveled down a long, winding driveway flanked by large, barren trees, the branches towering above them. Moonlight illuminated the dark winter sky down the path toward Huntly Manor. Liam stretched his arms over his head to alleviate the kinks in his stiff muscles. Lily's head bobbed on the side of the carriage, her dark curls escaping from her long braid. Noah gazed out the window of the carriage, a solemn look on his face.

"So we finally made it?" Liam asked.

"Yes."

"Should we wake Lily?"

"Probably a good idea; we'll be at the front door soon enough."

"I know why we did this, but my parents are going to go crazy once they figure out we left."

"That's the point, isn't it?"

Liam looked over at his sleeping sister and back at his friend. He didn't like what his father had done, but what about their own actions? Were they any better? Did they have the right to worry their parents with their rash actions? Now, after hours of travel, he'd had time to think about the situation. They might have acted carelessly and should have talked to their mother first. She wouldn't have allowed him to be forced into a betrothal contract. His mother was dead-set against forcing either one of them into an unwanted marriage.

"It was. I'm not so sure about this anymore."

"There's no going back now. We're at my ancestral home now. All we can do is sit back and wait. They'll be here soon enough and it will be settled."

Liam nodded. "I suppose you're right."

"Are we at Huntly Manor?" Lily lifted her head, her blue eyes still droopy from sleep.

The carriage came to a full stop. Liam looked out the window at a large towering manor. There were at least forty tapered steps leading to the front door. Large sections of it resembled a medieval castle.

"Why didn't you tell me you lived in a castle?" Lily exclaimed, excitement filling her voice.

"Yeah, all you need is a moat and drawbridge and you'll be living in ancient times," Liam joked.

With a dry, humorless tone, Noah explained, "They were removed a century ago when the stairs were crafted. They've done a bit of remodeling, my ancestors, to make it into more of manor instead of a castle. A lot of the main structure still stands, but it is as modernized as they could make it."

"You don't like it here, do you?" Lily asked in a quiet tone.

"Not so much. It's never been much of a happy place. My parents hated each other. The best times I've had have been at your home. Sometimes I don't think you two know how good you have it."

"I'm sorry, Noah. You don't talk about your parents much. Why didn't you ever tell me?" Liam asked.

"I don't like talking about it and I've already said too much. Let's go inside and wait for your parents to come get us. I hope they still allow me to spend Christmas with you."

"Of course they will. They adore you and they'll know it's not your fault. We can be a bit—difficult— to say no to." An impish smile formed on Lily's face.

They all hopped down from the carriage and walked inside Huntly manor. They were greeted by a surprised housekeeper. "Your Grace." She curtsied. "We weren't expecting you."

"My apologies, Molly, this was a bit last-minute. Can you get some rooms ready?"

"Certainly. How many will you be needing?"

"Besides mine? I suggest getting four ready. We'll probably be getting some extra guests soon."

"Right away, Your Grace." Molly nodded her head. "Will you be requiring anything else? Perhaps some refreshments?"

"No, we're rather tired; just prepare the rooms."

"Very well, Your Grace. I will gather a few maids and have them organize the chambers for you and your guests."

Molly left to get the rooms ready. Noah led Lily and Liam into the library. The butler had lit a fire to keep them warm as they waited. They sat back and relaxed on the chaises until they could retire to nice warm beds.

"How long until you think they'll arrive?" Lily asked.

"Knowing Father, they are probably not too far behind us. With any luck we'll be asleep in a nice warm bed and they'll leave us there until morning."

"Do you think they will?"

"Not bloody likely."

Liam studied his sister and best friend. What were they thinking, running off in the middle of the night? They'd be lucky if their parents didn't murder them. He sighed and leaned his head on the chaise. Nothing to do about it now; they just had to sit back and wait for disaster to strike.

PIA'S HEAD rested on Thor's shoulder. She finally gave into her exhaustion and allowed herself to get some rest. Thoughts kept whirling through his head, not allowing him the same luxury. He couldn't help praying he was right and that the twins had coerced the young Duke of Huntly into going to his country estate. The carriage rattled along the roadway, the dark sky lightening as the sun rose in the distance. They had wasted a lot of time traipsing around London trying to locate them. At the rate things were going they wouldn't make it to Huntly Manor until dawn broke.

Pia lifted her head from his shoulder and yawned. "How much longer until we arrive?"

"I'm guessing an hour at least. The sun's beginning to rise."

"Did you get any sleep?"

"No, I have too much on my mind."

Pia's eyes pinned him. She stared at him for several seconds, biting her lip as if deep in thought. Thor didn't know what was rolling through her mind. A part of him was terrified of the answer; she hadn't been happy with his actions of late. He'd really messed up, his dealings with the Earl of Devon playing havoc on his family. At least he knew he'd taken care of it and could reassure Liam he was not betrothed to marry Lady Gemma Kemsley.

"As you should; they wouldn't have run away if not for your actions," Pia retorted.

"I've had enough of this." Thor smacked the side of the carriage with his fist, a sharp sting spreading through his fingers. "Can you just let it go?"

"I'd rather not." Pia glared. "It's all that is keeping me focused right now."

Thor nodded. "I make an easy target, love, but you know me. Just try and see it from my point of view."

"You're right. I know you better than anyone." Pia folded her hands in her lap. "They're going to be fine. I can't keep blaming you. The twins are headstrong and it's hard to predict what they may or may not do."

"I set us on this course and I do know what my actions caused. I'm responsible for their rash actions."

Pia placed her hand on his shoulder and stared into his eyes. "You're right; you did, but you didn't tell those two to run away. They did that all on their own. If they had bothered to think, they'd realize you wouldn't have gone through with that betrothal contract."

"I know, but I can't help feeling the guilt. It should never have existed. Drinking in excess is no excuse. We both feel the same way. We want our children to be happy and dictating who they choose to marry isn't going to give them any kind of joy."

"I love you, Thor."

"I love you, too."

Thor pulled Pia into his arms and placed his lips on hers. She opened her mouth, allowing him full access. His tongue rolled over hers with gentle swirls. His hand cupped her cheek as he deepened the kiss. Thor pulled back and stared into her blue eyes. He reached down and scooped her fully into his lap and began trailing kisses down her throat and across her shoulders. A soft moan escaped Pia's mouth. Thor could feel himself begin to harden as desire flooded him. He would never get enough of his wife. He always wanted her, and he needed to be inside of her. She reached down and undid his breeches as he lifted her skirts and settled them around his lap. Pia lowered herself on his length, engulfing him in her warm passage. Once he was deep inside her, she began to ride him, up and down in slow, agonizing strokes. Thor rested his hands on her hips, guiding her to go faster, until he could feel her channel start to ripple with the onslaught of her orgasm. He could feel his own orgasm begin to crest as her inner muscles gripped him. Soon it exploded through him, draining him of energy. He groaned as pleasure washed over him in waves. Pia's head fell forward, resting on his shoulder. He wrapped his arms around her and held on tightly, his member still buried inside of her.

"We haven't made love in a carriage in a very long time."

"We probably shouldn't be doing it now."

"Why not?" she asked. "I wanted you, and you clearly wanted me. I don't see anything wrong with what we just did."

"Our children are missing—"

"But not for long. We're almost to Huntly. We'll

deal with our naughty children when we reach them."

A small weight lifted off his shoulders with his wife's reassuring embrace. They would find them and in the meantime they could enjoy each other for the remainder of the long journey to Huntly Manor.

"You're awfully sure about this, love." A warm, yet cocky smile formed on his face.

"Because nothing can go wrong now." She lifted her head and lightly touched her lips to his. "You're ready for another round, aren't you?"

"Well, we do have a little time..."

They began all over again, and Thor allowed himself to just enjoy loving his wife. Their children would feel their wrath when they caught up to them, but the worry dissipated with the assurance they were fine at the young Duke's estate.

CHAPTER FOUR

*T*he sun began to stream through the windows of the bedroom Liam had been assigned at Huntly Manor, bright enough to wake him from a sound sleep. He sat up and rubbed the sleepy fog from his eyes. His gaze fell on the window.

"Should've remembered to close the curtains," he said to himself.

The bedroom door creaked open and Noah stepped inside. Tired from their journey, Liam noticed they both decided to sleep in their clothes, leaving them a rumpled mess. "I thought I might find you awake. I was so tired last night I forgot to close the curtains. As we were all exhausted, I thought perhaps you had forgotten to as well. I see your room is equally as bright as mine."

"Yeah, it sure is. Any chance we can get breakfast this early?"

Noah nodded his head. "Indeed, they are already preparing it. Should we retrieve Lily?"

"Yeah, we have a bit to discuss, though you should be prepared. Lily can sleep through anything and will be quite irritated at being awoken so early."

"I can handle it; I've grown accustomed to Lily's moods from visiting your house the past year."

Liam nodded and got up to follow Noah to Lily's room. They opened the door to find her sound asleep on the bed, the room completely dark. Lily had remembered to close her curtains. She liked her sleep and apparently had enough forethought to remember the possibility of early sunshine streaming through the window. Liam walked across the room and spread the curtains wide to allow the bright light to cascade into the room. It fell in quick succession across Lily's face, illuminating her dark curls, and her wrinkled blue dress. In sleep, she appeared angelic, but Liam knew how devilish his sister could be. The brilliant glow of sunshine was not doing much to awaken her, so he walked over to her bed and began to push on her shoulder. Lily jolted upright, her eyes flying open as they landed on Liam.

"Why are you waking me up? Are Mother and Father here?"

Liam shook his head. "No. We are going down for breakfast and we need you to join us."

"How early is it? I feel like I haven't slept at all."

"It's still quite early, you probably only slept four hours or so." Noah's quiet voice entered the room from his place just inside the doorframe of Lily's room.

"Do we really need to get up this early?" Lily asked.

"Yes, I'm sure we will have visitors soon." Liam held his hand out to his sister to assist her from the bed. "Come on, let's go eat."

They followed Noah down to the small dining room and sat at the table. The servants began to serve them a light breakfast of poached eggs, bacon, and freshly baked bread. Liam picked up a slice of bread and spread creamy butter across it and set it on the plate of food the servant set in front of him. He no sooner picked up his fork to take a bite when the sound of voices interrupted him.

"Ah, there you three are. See, Thor, I told you

they would be fine. I hope you had a nice adventure; it is going to be your last for several years to come."

His father glared at his mother and just shook his head back and forth in a slow motion. Liam watched his parents enter the room and take a seat at the dining table. Once they were both sitting, they turned their attention back to the three of them.

"So it looks like we have some things to discuss," his father said, folding his hands across his chest.

"Yes, sir." Liam nodded his head. "Indeed we do."

"You know you could have saved us all some time and just come to talk to me." Thor glowered at Liam.

"I didn't think of it at the time. I—we just reacted."

"Yes, have you had time to think about your actions and what they mean?" Pia asked them.

Liam could feel a well of emotions begin to roll through him. He still didn't want to marry some girl he'd never met. He could feel anger build up inside of him again. How could his father have done that to him? His arms folded across his chest defensively, he expressed his discontent. "You know why we left. I don't want to marry the Earl of Devon's daughter. I don't even know her. I'd like the chance to marry someone I love, if I marry at all."

"Liam, dear, you do know I wouldn't have

allowed that to happen," his mother reassured him. "You shouldn't have run off."

Liam wouldn't regret his choices. He couldn't change them even if he wanted to. "I know that now, but I can't undo it." Anger and fury flowed through him as he stared his father in the eyes.

"There will be repercussions. We can't have you running off because you're scared. We need you to understand you can talk to us about anything, no matter how difficult the subject." Thor hammered home his point by pinning all three of them down with his gaze. "If you had bothered to ask, you would know I didn't sign the contract with the Earl of Devon. You are not going to be forced to marry anyone. It will always be your choice. I made a mistake and I apologize for it."

Liam lowered his head as the weight of his actions fell over him. He worried his parents and stressed over something that wouldn't have been an issue. He acted rashly. "I'm sorry, I promise I won't run away again. I will face whatever is bothering me. It is cowardly to think running will solve my problems."

The servants came in and set plates of breakfast in front of his parents, along with some silverware. His mother picked up her fork and began to cut her egg. His father continued to look across the table at them all.

"Liam isn't the only one at fault here." Lily began to play with her napkin, twisting it into a ball between her fingers. "I'm sorry too. Liam is right we shouldn't have run away."

Liam looked at his friend. He didn't say a word during the entire exchange. Noah didn't show an ounce of emotion. He continued to stare at Liam's father. When it mattered most to Noah, his emotions ran more deeply and he showed none. Liam learned his friend's biggest fear was losing those individuals he'd come to love most. They now included his entire family, and he didn't want to be cast off.

"Sir, I apologize for our actions. What do you plan to do?" Noah asked.

"I plan on eating some breakfast and then dragging you three back to London. Tomorrow is Christmas and we still have not decorated the tree. The servants should have it set up in the sitting room by now so we can direct our attention to it when we get home."

Surprise filled Noah's face. "You're going to allow me to come back with you?"

"Of course. Why would I punish you solely for all

of your actions? However, there will be punishments meted out once I decide on the proper ones."

"Now, all of you eat. We have a long day ahead," Liam's mother ordered them.

Not long after they were done with breakfast, they grabbed their reticules, and all of them sat in a carriage for the long journey home. Fresh horses harnessed to the carriage had been swapped with those in Huntly's stable. They were exhausted, but anxious to return to London.

IT WAS early afternoon when they arrived at Marsden House, and the kids went to their chambers to rest before dinner. The Christmas festivities would start after they had eaten the evening meal. Thor followed Pia up to her chamber and closed the door behind them. He wanted to spend some extra quality time with her alone. Their argument was well over with and set aside on their journey to retrieve the children. He pulled off his jacket, folded it, and placed it on a chair near the door.

A gamine smile on her face, Pia tilted her head and stared at him. "Do you need something?"

"Yes."

She raised an eyebrow and crossed her arms beneath her generous bosom. "What can I do for you?"

Thor began to undo his cravat, pulled it off his neck, and tossed it aside. "I need you, love." He pulled his shirt off next and tossed it in the opposite direction of the cravat. His breeches undone and hanging low on his hips, he stalked Pia.

Pia took a step back. "You're not tired?"

"I'm never too tired to make love to my beautiful wife."

Thor continued to move forward as Pia stepped back. She hit the bed and fell backward onto it. He kneeled beside her, towering over her small frame. Reaching up, she ran her hands over his bare, muscled torso and squeezed one of his erect nipples. Thor reacted by lifting her skirts and skimming his hands across her thighs.

"You have too many clothes on." Lifting Pia up, he pushed her bodice down, revealing her lush breasts resting on top of her corset. Thor licked her pink nipple and nipped at it, repeating the action with the other one. He hoisted her up off the bed and turned her around. His hands roamed across her back as he undid the laces of her dress and corset, pushing her chemise over her shoulders. Thor spun her back around and pushed all of her clothing down in one full sweep. He trailed his eyes over her naked flesh. Pia shivered and Thor could see her body begin to flush with desire. Thor picked her back up and placed her beside him on the bed. He continued to lick, nip, and kiss her whole body.

"Enough. I need you inside me," Pia demanded.

Thor stood and pushed his breeches off. He spread Pia's legs, pulled her forward, and pushed his thick member deep into her. Pia moaned as her channel rippled around his length. Pia squeezed him with her inner muscles. Thor bit his lip as the pleasure raked over his sensitive flesh. He had to rein in his control and ease into loving her. If she kept stroking him with the muscles in her tight channel he would ravage her. He set a slow pace, stroking himself in and out of her. Pia raked her nails across his chest and moaned. Thor began to push himself in and out of her with deep rapid strokes. Pia's breathing became shallow and rapid; Thor could feel her orgasm begin as she squeezed against him. She screamed when she went over the edge. Thor moaned and threw his head back as his seed emptied inside of her. Afterwards he pulled himself out of her warmth and stood up. Thor lifted her up into his arms so he could pull down the bed sheets, and placed her on the bed. He crawled in beside her and spread the sheets over top of them. Thor pulled Pia into his arms; she curled into him and rested her head on his shoulder.

"I think I can sleep now," he whispered in her ear.

"I should hope so." Pia's laugh was light and throaty.

"Remind me when we wake up I have a special present for you."

"What if I want it now?"

"I'm too exhausted, love. You undo me. It can wait."

A pout formed on her face at his words. "You can be awful sometimes."

"Me? Never, wicked, on the other hand..." Thor began to trail his fingers over her erect nipples.

"I thought you were too tired?" Pia gasped as his fingers trailed down her hips and began to play with the tiny sensitive nub near her entrance. She moaned while his fingers stroked over her heated flesh. He could feel her begin to squirm beneath him.

"I believe I said I'm never too tired to make love to my wife."

Thor kissed her, pushing his tongue inside her

mouth, effectively distracting her from the conversation about her present. He began to stroke her center with his fingers, rubbing over the sensitive tip, causing Pia to gasp. Deciding to distract her further, he roamed down to kiss her center. He spread her thighs and replaced his fingers with his tongue. Pia wrapped her legs over his shoulders, bringing herself closer to his wicked tongue. He began to push his fingers inside of her, caressing her channel as his tongue massaged the sensitive area of her sex. Thor licked and sucked her until he could feel her explode around his fingers. He pushed her legs off his shoulders and spread them wide. Then he crawled on top of her, pushing himself deep inside her. He began to pound into her with furious thrusts, desperate for his own release. He hadn't lied to her; he would never have enough of her, and he was always ready to make love with her. He needed her like he needed air to breathe. If not for her, he would still be a pirate roaming the seas for treasure. Pia, his sexy, flawed, perfect jewel, the angel he never thought to find in life. His orgasm hit him as he reveled in her beauty. A few minutes later he rolled off her and wrapped her tightly in his embrace once again.

"Sleep, love, we have a busy evening planned."

Pia's eyes drifted closed. Thor watched her for several seconds before he began to feel his own eyes drift closed.

CHAPTER FIVE

*T*hor led Pia into the sitting room, where he found all three children sitting on the settee, patiently waiting for them to arrive.

"Oh good, you're finally here," Lily exclaimed.

Liam watched them with apprehensive eyes. Thor could tell his child didn't know what to expect from them. He still needed to punish them for their behavior, but hadn't thought of what would be the proper chastisement for their actions. The children needed to stew for a little while as he mulled over his options; once he decided on a proper punishment he would let them know.

"Are you in a hurry for your punishment?" Thor asked her.

"Um, no, I thought we were going to decorate the

tree..." Fear filled Lily's eyes as she stared at him. Good, she needed to know he hadn't forgotten their rash behavior.

"Did you decide what you're going to do with us?" Liam asked.

Thor looked over at his son. Resignation filled his eyes. He was ready and willing to accept whatever punishment Thor planned on assigning them.

"I will get to it in a minute."

"We have a few other things to discuss with you first," Pia explained.

Thor and Pia walked fully into the room and sat on a settee opposite the children. All three of them stared back at them, their eyes wide and curious.

"As you can see the tree is set up and ready to decorate." Pia gestured towards the tree the servants had cut down and placed inside the sitting room. "We will get to it in a moment. First we want to discuss your birthday."

Liam's eyebrows rose as he looked over at Lily. "What about it?"

"We were planning a special surprise for you, but in light of your actions we have decided against it," Thor explained.

A glum expression formed on both of the twins' faces. Thor didn't want to disappoint them, but believed they hadn't earned the planned surprise.

"We were going to get you a carriage of your own to share. A little phaeton I was planning on teaching you both to drive; however, in light of your penchant for running away I've decided against it."

"But Father..." Lily began to say before Liam interrupted her.

"No, Lily. Father's right. I don't think we've earned the responsibility. Maybe in a couple of years, but we're too young."

Lily nodded her head at Liam and turned her attention back to Thor and Pia. "I understand. Liam's right, besides I'd probably only get in more trouble with my own carriage."

"So we will have to give you a less expensive birthday present."

Lily looked at them both expectantly. "We're still getting presents?"

"Yes and no," Pia explained.

"You still have your Christmas gifts," Thor offered.

Pia nodded. "Indeed. Our gift for your birthday is to allow you to even have a Christmas."

Both Liam and Lily groaned.

"We could cancel all of the festivities," Thor reminded them.

"No, please don't," Lily begged.

During the entire exchange Thor noticed how Noah watched and waited. He didn't know what to make of the young duke. His reserved demeanor made him feel sad. He had lost so much at a young age.

"What about you, Noah?"

"I don't understand, sir?"

"Do you still want to have the Christmas festivities?"

"I'm just glad you're allowing me to be a part of your family." Noah's voice was quiet and heavy with emotion.

"Son, you know you're welcome here anytime," Thor reminded him.

Pia held her hand over her heart, tears forming in the corners of her eyes. "Noah, don't ever feel like you're not welcome here."

Noah's head bobbed back and forth between the two of them. After several seconds he gave them a formal nod. "I won't."

Time ticked by while they talked and Thor considered how to discipline them. After they were well into the discussion, Thor decided the exact punishment to give them for their misbehaviors. He didn't want something too harsh; yet at the same time nothing equally too lenient.

"Now for your punishment," Thor began. "Each of you is going to help the maids clean for the next week. Expect to get up at dawn to assist them."

Another groan filled the room. "Unless you want more work..."

"No, Father, we'll help the maids," Liam offered before Thor could assign more tasks.

"Good, I will inform them of your duties and you're to listen to them. If even one maid comes to me with a bad report I'll make things infinitely worse. Do you all understand?"

Three heads nodded at him in agreement.

"All right. Lily and Liam, show Noah where the decorations are and we can begin trimming the tree," Pia ordered.

All three of the children hopped up and headed toward the box of decorations. With glee they began to hang up the various ornaments they collected over the past several years. Thor watched them as they hung each one up with care. Happiness radiating across their faces, they opened up each ornament and remembered when they picked it out.

"Don't you have a special gift for me?" Pia asked.

"Ah yes, I forgot."

"You did tell me to remind you."

"Indeed I did and then I got distracted."

A blush filled Pia's cheeks. "I remember how you became distracted."

His lips tilted into a smile filled with sin. "We'll have to become distracted in a similar fashion later."

"Yes, but now give me my present."

Thor looked over at his children and their friend. The tree was almost completely flowing with sparkling decorations as they continued to hang them on the green branches. Thor walked over and picked up a package near the box of decorations. It was adorned with the glittery dust of broken glass, ground down into fine grains and adhered to the sides of the box. It gave the impression of a thousand diamonds sparkling on the hard surface. A bright blue bow, matching the color of Pia's eyes, was wrapped around it. He picked it up, crossed back to his wife's side, and handed it to her.

She clapped her hands as joy spread across her face. "What is it?"

"Open it up and see."

Pia undid the ribbon with care and pulled it aside, letting it drift to the floor. She lifted the lid and gasped. Inside, against red plush velvet lay a crystal angel. A shiny gold halo floating above her head, gossamer wings spread high on her back, and her skirts hollow and fine, she shimmered much like the diamond sparkle on the package.

"Oh, Thor, she's beautiful."

"It's a special tree topper I had made for you. She's delicate, so we need to be careful when we place her on the tree. If she falls she could break rather easily."

"Will she stay in place?" Pia asked.

"Yes, there are a couple of hooks under her skirt to tie her down. When the children are done I'll help you place it on the highest branch. She's our own guardian angel to watch over us each Christmas."

"How lovely, thank you. I shall treasure her always."

Thor reached down and placed a soft kiss on Pia's lips. The children finished decorating the tree and turned their attention back on them.

"What's that?" Lily asked.

"A gift from your father," Pia explained as she turned toward Lily and Liam. "Are you ready to put it on the tree?"

"Yes," they both exclaimed.

Pia looked at Thor. "You're going to have to place

it on the tree, as you're the only one tall enough to reach the top."

Thor nodded and followed her over to the tall, fragrant pine. They placed the crystal angel on top and anchored her to the branches surrounding it. She gleamed down on them from her vantage point. Thor turned to look at his family and happiness welled up inside of him. His life couldn't have been more perfect if he tried. He looked back up at the crystal angel and smiled. Now they had a guardian angel to watch over them, a protective shield against any danger. He pulled Pia into his arms and stroked her hair with his hand. She was his living, breathing angel, and the twins their beautiful blessing.

ABOUT THE AUTHOR

USA TODAY Bestselling author, DAWN BROWER writes both historical and contemporary romance. There are always stories inside her head; she just never thought she could make them come to life. That creativity has finally found an outlet.

Growing up she was the only girl out of six children. She raised two boys into productive young men. There is never a dull moment in her life. Reading books is her favorite hobby and she loves all genres.

She is active on Facebook, Twitter, and Instagram. To follow her or can find more about her check out her website for the pertinent information:

www.authordawnbrower.com

If It's Love (Amanda Mariel)

Odds of Love (Dawn Brower)

Believe In Love (Amanda Mariel)

Chance of Love (Dawn Brower)

Love and Holly (Amanda Mariel)

Love and Mistletoe (Dawn Brower

Bluestockings Defying Rogues

When An Earl Turns Wicked

A Lady Hoyden's Secret

One Wicked Kiss

Earl In Trouble

All the Ladies Love Coventry

One Less Scandalous Earl

Confessions of a Hellion

Coming Soon

The Vixen in Red

Marsden Descendants

Rebellious Angel

Tempting An American Princess

How to Kiss a Debutante

Loving an America Spy

Marsden Romances

A Flawed Jewel

A Crystal Angel

A Treasured Lily

A Sanguine Gem

A Hidden Ruby

A Discarded Pearl

Novak Springs

Cowgirl Fever

Dirty Proof

Unbridled Pursuit

Sensual Games

Christmas Temptation

Linked Across Time

Saved by My Blackguard

Searching for My Rogue

Seduction of My Rake

Surrendering to My Spy

Spellbound by My Charmer

Stolen by My Knave

Separated from My Love

Scheming with My Duke

Secluded with My Hellion

Coming Soon

Secrets of My Beloved

Spying on My Scoundrel

Shocked by My Vixen

Heart's Intent

One Heart to Give

Unveiled Hearts

Heart of the Moment

Kiss My Heart Goodbye

Heart in Waiting

Broken Curses

The Enchanted Princess

The Bespelled Knight

The Magical Hunt

Ever Beloved

Forever My Earl

Always My Viscount

Infinitely My Marquess

EternallyMyDuke

Kismet Bay

Once Upon a Christmas

New Year Revelation

All Things Valentine

Luck At First Sight

Endless Summer Days

A Witch's Charm

All Out of Gratitude

Christmas Ever After

AFTERWORD

Thank you so much for taking the time to read my book.

Your opinion matters!

Please take a moment to review this book on your favorite review site and share your opinion with fellow readers.

www.authordawnbrower.com

ACKNOWLEDGMENTS

Thanks Victoria Miller. You're the best.

EXCERPT: A FLAWED JEWEL

A MARSDEN ROMANCE BOOK ONE

DAWN BROWER

USA TODAY
BESTSELLING AUTHOR

Dawn Brower

A MARSDEN
ROMANCE

A Flawed Jewel

March 3, 1861

"You need to suck in more, Miss Pieretta."

Tully, her maid prodded and pulled at the strings of Pieretta's corset to tighten it as much as possible. One of many torturous things a lady must endure to remain fashionable. It was her job to get Pieretta ready for the biggest voyage of her life. There was nothing Pieretta wanted more than to stay on the plantation where she grew up, but her presence was required at her grandpere's estate in France. She had no real desire to go anywhere. Everything she knew was in Charleston. She had no choice but to go live in a country she knew nothing about.

Tully yanked on the laces one last time squeezing Pieretta's ribs tightly inside her chest. She struggled to breathe. Pieretta squirmed in an effort to loosen the stays. "Miss Pieretta, please, we need to tighten this corset a little more, or you will never fit into that traveling dress you had the seamstress make for you. We all know you're only stalling so you don't have to leave the plantation. Your grandpere is expecting you, and you need to be on that ship."

"Oh be quiet, Tully. The laces are too tight. Fix them before I can no longer breathe." Stupid know-it-all maid thought she could order her around. It was bad enough that her entire life was about to change. Now she had to deal with Tully ordering her around. "The dress will fit and still allow air to enter my lungs. Mind your own business and do as you're told," Pieretta scolded her.

As a southern belle, she didn't have to do anything more than host parties and help her father manage the house. The most traveling she had ever done was to attend picnics and soirees at neighboring plantations. She had never traveled more than fifteen miles away from her home. The idea of sailing all the way to France—Pia hated to admit it, but it terrified her.

Pieretta had never boarded a ship, now she was expected to sale on a long voyage. She, at least, had seen one or two while they were in the Charleston harbor, but it had never crossed her mind ever to give one a closer look. It was not an experience she ever expected to have.

Her happiest moments were in Charleston, in the heart of the only home she had ever known.

Pieretta didn't want to leave everything behind. It was hard to comprehend why her grandpere insisted she come live with him in France. The fact she didn't have any living male relatives in Charleston shouldn't matter. She could look after the plantation and deal with the overseer. Her father made sure she understood every aspect of running the plantation. She had the best education possible. He believed females had a right to learn more than just how to run a household or proper etiquette.

Oh, Papa, I miss you so much...

A sting of pain hit her chest. She was reminded again of her father's death a month ago. Each day without her father was more unbearable than the one before it. Pieretta couldn't believe she had to live in a world where he no longer existed. His death had been so sudden—had suddenly just quit breathing. It had been so devastating to realize someone could die without any warning.

Pieretta was all alone in the world.

She had no brothers or sisters, and her only living relative was her grandpere. So it was with a heavy heart that she prepared to make the journey to live with him in France.

Her mother died when Pieretta was born, and her father never remarried. He loved her mother too much to ever envision a life with someone else. The only females Pieretta spent time around on a regular basis were servants. Without the benefit of a maternal influence, Pieretta had more masculine ideas about her future. It would have been all right to stay and run the plantation if she had been a man, but as a woman, she had no real say in her life until she reached her majority.

Until then, her grandpere, Comte Renard Dubois, had the right to tell her how to live her life.

Because she had never been to France, she didn't know what to expect once she arrived. Grandpere had told her stories about his estate and how large it was, but she had never had the opportunity to visit. He outlined the many gardens and the different foliage that it encased. Pieretta looked forward to walking amongst the roses and counting the various shades his gardener cultivated.

She had never seen an actual rose, but her grand-pere's description made them sound like the most beautiful flower on Earth. The blossoms were rumored to be filled with an aromatic scent that tantalized the nose. Rose buds bloomed in a variety of colors from the shade of a blushing bride's cheeks to the various hues of sunshine bouncing through the windows of her sitting room. Even with the allure of seeing roses for the first time, she still had no desire to travel such a long distance.

All of her trunks were packed and already aboard the ship. The only thing required of her now was to get herself ready, get in the carriage, and travel to the docks.

Pieretta wanted to throw a fit and stomp her feet, but that would be out of character for her. While her father often indulged her, Pieretta was not prone to temper tantrums. She did occasionally let her displeasure be known, but most of the time she was able to hold back the temptation to scream. Pieretta took a deep breath and exhaled slowly, preparing herself for whatever the journey might entail.

She stood up straight as Tully finished tying the corset's laces. She didn't want to stand still any longer than necessary and keeping still ensured the bows on her dress were tied evenly.

In her mind, fighting the inevitable would not help her situation. The servants needed to make sure she made it on the ship. Even though Pieretta didn't to move to France, she could make the best of the situation. Her life on the plantation had a repetitive quality to it—nothing ever changed.

Instead of harping on the negative, she could look at this forced trip as an adventure.

"Almost done, Miss Pieretta."

"It's taking forever," she groaned. Sometimes being female was a nuisance. Surely it didn't take this long for a man to get dressed.

"It'll be all done before you know it and then we will be boarding a ship to France."

Did Tully have to give her a reminder of it?

Tully finished lacing her stays, and the corset hugged every curve of her torso. She walked over and picked up Pieretta's traveling gown and opened it for Pieretta to step into. Once she was fully within the confines of the dress, Tully pulled it up and began the long process of latching all of the hooks up the side. She opted not to wear any petticoats or a hoop skirt, as it would be ridiculous to wear them in the small confines of the ship. Her traveling costume was made of the finest dyed black wool.

Black Wool was ever so dull and boring, but Pia didn't mind wearing it to honor her father. She'd miss him for the rest of her days. When she received the letter from her grandpere, Pieretta visited her favorite seamstress to have a few traveling costumes made for her crossing to France. She had no idea what the current fashion was and figured more gowns could be made upon her arrival at her grandpere's estate.

Besides only so much could be done to make a black gown look good...

She was trying to be practical, and Grandpere wouldn't mind. He would want his little princess to be happy. After all, one couldn't be happy if one wasn't fashionable. Grandpere believed she didn't have the brains for anything besides frivolous things such as fashion. He did not realize Pieretta had a lot of things on her mind, and fashion wasn't always at the forefront.

Soon he'd realize how mistaken he was about her character.

For instance, her love of mythology consumed her. Some of her favorite books housed stories of the gods and how they had fallen. She read everything from Norse to Greek mythology. Her favorite had always been Thor. Pieretta often wished she could visit Asgard and have the opportunity to meet him and Loki.

"Tully, please tell me you remembered to pack my favorite books."

"Yes, ma'am" Tully nodded. "You have more books packed than you do gowns."

"Books are more important."

"hmmph" Tully snorted. "I wouldn't know as I've never had the opportunity to learn to read."

"Maybe I will teach you on our voyage. Not like we have anything better to occupy our time with."

"I don't know how much use I'd have for learning." Tully frowned. "Why don't we just wait and see how the crossing goes. You might find something to entertain yourself with."

Pieretta sighed. No one truly understood her— especially her only living relative.

Grandpere knew next to nothing about what Pieretta actually liked. He assumed she was similar to her mother, Dominique Dubois Carlyle, who only thought of frivolous things such as the latest styles and idle gossip.

Her grandpere couldn't be more wrong.

He usually visited her at least twice a year,

staying for a few weeks and then returning home. Her mother was his original princess. Grandpere had doted on her his whole life. When her mother died, he had been heartbroken. When he saw his new granddaughter with her mother's royal blue eyes and pale blond hair, he had decided that he had a new princess to coddle with affection. It had helped to ease the sting of his loss, finding a near carbon copy of his beloved daughter. He'd found a way to fill the empty hole in his heart with Pieretta.

Tully finished connecting all of the hooks on Pieretta's dress. She inspected her work, trailing her fingers over the dress to smooth the lines. Stepping away, Tully motioned for Pieretta to sit down on the chair next to her vanity. "Miss Pieretta, you need to sit down so I can fix your hair."

She had no idea what Tully meant by fix her hair. She hadn't touched it. "What are you going to do to my hair, Tully?" Pieretta asked.

"Don't you worry any, Miss Pieretta. I am just going to pull it back a bit so it's out of your way. You're not going to want to deal with it on that there ship. It needs to be more manageable."

Pieretta sighed and sat in front of her vanity. Unfortunately, she had to deal with Tully even though she was a meddlesome nuisance. Tully had helped raise her, the servant believed she had a right to dictate how Pieretta should live her life. Tully's many lectures were a normal part of her day. In Pieretta's mind, Tully was overstepping her duties and trying to take the place of the mother she never knew. The maid was traveling with her only because a young unmarried lady could not travel alone. She was going to be the only person Pieretta would bring with her into this new life.

"I suppose you're right," Pieretta agreed. "It would be rather tiresome to constantly push my hair out of the way."

"Trust me, I know what I'm talking about."

Pieretta rolled her eyes. "Oh? And exactly how many ships have you sailed on?"

"I haven't always been on this plantation," Tully informed her. "I came over here on a ship when I was a tiny thing. Of course, my hair didn't have the opportunity to get blown around, but I do remember the howling winds."

"Howling winds?" Pieretta gulped. "What do you mean?"

"There was a nasty bit of storm for half the journey. The winds whipped right through the ship leaving an eerie whistling piercing our ears."

That didn't sound—appealing.

Tully pulled Pieretta's braid tighter and wrapped it around her head. Pieretta sighed, fighting tears as Tully continued to plait her hair. It was difficult to keep her emotions from welling up and spilling out of her. If she had one wish, it would be to find a way out of the situation her grandpere had forced her into. Her only option wasn't really an option in her mind. She could get married, but she didn't want any person to have that sort of power over her life. Relinquishing control meant fighting for the right to make any decisions for herself. Marriage was the one thing Pieretta had never wanted.

When she turned twenty-five, she would gain control of the plantation. It would be a long seven years living with her grandpere, but if anyone could do it, she could. Pieretta had to make sure her grandpere knew she was never going to get married. In Pieretta's mind, any woman had the capability to make her own decisions. It would be a cold day in hell before she allowed a man to have any kind of control over her life or her inheritance. Her father had made sure she was educated far beyond her station, and she had a working knowledge. She was intelligent and intended to use everything she learned to further her ambitions.

Tully finished fussing with her hair. Her pale

blond locks were now securely wound around her head in a practical plait. Pieretta brushed a tear from the corner of her eye. Would she ever be happy again? She had serious doubts that happiness lay in her future. Pieretta stood and flattened her dress, smoothing the lines and wrinkles along the side of her skirt so it fell evenly as she moved. She glanced in the mirror. The dress wasn't designed to be flattering, but Pieretta believed she could make anything look good. She may be pale and sad, but she was still beautiful. She was curvy in all the right places with a small waist.

"All right, Tully, I guess now is as good a time as any," Pieretta said. "Go and have the carriage brought around. I'm ready for an adventure. That's how I'm choosing to see this change in my life."

Eerie winds and all...

Pieretta stood and looked around her bedroom one last time. Several years would pass before she could return and take control of the plantation. It was important that she store all of the good memories so the years in France would be easier to bear.

The fight to gain control over her life would be tough, but the things that mattered the most were worth fighting for. Even though at times she felt like she would never be happy again, Pieretta had hoped that she would find a reason to smile. Changes were always hard to make.

She wandered over to her bedroom door and pulled it open. She began the long trek down the stairs to the main hallway. At the bottom of the steps, she looked up as Tully made her way down the long staircase. No one ever promised life would be easy, and if Pieretta knew one thing, it was that she could get through any hurdle life put in her way. This was only one bump on a very long road ahead of her, but in the end, she knew she would get what she wanted. After all, Pieretta always did.

THE DOCKS WERE NOT a pleasant place to walk. They were filthy and smelled of unimaginable things. The scent of rotten fish and fresh salt water permeated the air. Pieretta needed to board the ship as quickly as possible, before she stepped in something disgusting.

The waterfront was booming with activity, and the noise was deafening. It was hard to ascertain the different sounds and locate where they might be coming from. The combination of the odors stung her nose and throat. The smoky air made her eyes water. Pieretta covered her nose with her hand in an effort to block out the stench but was forced to wipe the tears from her eyes as they started to stream down her face. Tully followed behind her as fast as she could. They both wanted off the docks as fast as they could manage it.

"Miss Pieretta, we need to move faster. I don't like it on these docks. Some of those men are making me uneasy. They're looking at us like we're a special treat they want to lap up."

"Don't be ridiculous Tully, they wouldn't dare harm us. We'll be fine. Just the same, there's our ship. Let's board quickly and be done with this area."

A lump formed in her throat. She gulped it down and refrained from looking at the men Tully referred to. They made her just as uneasy, but she refused to admit it.

They moved quickly to the gangplank so they could board the clipper. The ship had three large masts each filled to the top with five sails. When they stepped on deck, the first mate and captain greeted them.

The captain folded one of his hands behind his back with the other one tucked in front just below his chest and bowed to Pieretta. "It's a pleasure to have you aboard, Miss Carlyle. I am Captain

Devere, and this is my first mate, Cam. I know Comte Dubois is anxiously awaiting your arrival in France."

"Do you know my grandpere well then?"

"As this is one of his ships, I have had many occasions to spend time with him, discussing how his shipments are to be handled. You are one of our most important cargos. He made sure to have a meeting with me before I left France and gave me the strictest instructions regarding your safety on this crossing."

Did he? She shouldn't be surprised, and yet she was.

"Grandpere can be very protective. I'm surprised he didn't make the trip himself."

"He wanted to, but an emergency arose at the last minute on one of his estates. It was something that required his personal attention. It is why he gave me instructions as to your passage and care. I hope your crossing with us is pleasant."

Pleasant? As far as she was concerned, there really wasn't anything that could make this journey tolerable let alone pleasurable. It took every ounce of her will to not come back with a rude comment. The need to get to her cabin and rest was starting to become a top priority to Pieretta. She needed to vacate the captain's company with as much haste as possible.

With as much politeness as she could muster, she cleared her throat. "I certainly wouldn't want it to be unpleasant. Who is to show us to our cabin?"

"My first mate will gladly give you a brief tour of the ship and show you to your cabin. We would prefer you remain in your quarters for most of the trip. It is the safest option. We will have a tray brought to you for all of your meals."

Was the captain mad? How could he expect me to be confined to a small room for three weeks? She would have to make her needs known from the very beginning or be stifled inside of a cabin with Tully for the lengthy passage. Her throat closed up just at the thought of it—she hated being confined.

"I couldn't possibly stay locked inside a small room the entire journey, Captain. We are going to be on the ship for at least two weeks. I would go mad for sure. I must insist on daily walks above deck."

The captain studied her for several seconds before he nodded.

"Very well, but limit them to thirty minute intervals twice a day. Do not walk on deck once night falls for any reason. If I tell you to get below deck, you are not to argue. Just go. I wouldn't insist unless it was a matter of safety."

"I can agree to that."

"Very well, Cam will see you to your cabin now."

The first mate guided Tully and Pieretta below deck and escorted them to their accommodations. There wasn't a lot of free space aboard the ship. The captain gave his quarters to the two women for the trip. Pieretta wondered where the captain would stay during the crossing to France. It would be cramped for all those involved.

Pieretta sighed as she entered the cabin. The limited space didn't leave much room for her to share with her maid. The journey across the ocean stuck in such a tightly confined room with Tully constantly telling her what to do might drive her mad. Tully scrambled in behind her, scuffling her feet as she settled into the small room. If only Grandpere hadn't demanded she come live with him. Why must females be dependent on their male relations?

"Thank you, sir. I think we will be fine for now. How long until we set sail?"

"If all goes well, we should be on our way in an hour's time. Please remain here for the rest of the evening. It will be too dark to walk on deck, and it is easy to fall overboard when you can't see in front of you."

"I will heed your advice, sir. I have no desire to swim, or sink, any time soon." Pieretta shuddered.

As the first mate left the two women, Pieretta only had one thought. *It's going to be a very long and grueling excursion across the immense ocean.*

EXCERPT: A TREASURED LILY

A MARSDEN ROMANCE BOOK TWO

DAWN BROWER

Dawn Brower

A Treasured Lily

CHAPTER 1

"*I* just don't think it's a good idea."

"Nonsense." Lilliana Marsden looked up at her best friend, Lady Gemma Kemsley, and frowned. "It's a brilliant idea. My father is being unreasonable about allowing me to travel to America. The plantation in South Carolina is my inheritance. It's about time I claimed it."

"It's not going to work for you to just show up and claim it though. I don't get why you are in such a hurry. You know full well you won't inherit it until you marry." Gemma reached up and smoothed over her sanguine curls, tucking a loose strand behind her ear.

"Well, that's not entirely true." Lilliana's lips twitched into a cheeky smile; it helped to have a little insight into how her parents worked. Gemma didn't know how much she'd gotten away with over the years. Eavesdropping had become a habit of hers. A person could find out the most interesting things quite by accident. When she overheard her parent's most recent conversation she couldn't help the glee that filled her soul. Reining in her excitement had taken an enormous amount of restraint. She needed to leave England and start the life she envisioned for herself. One she had complete control over. Her parent's still hoped she would settle down and get married, but they didn't know her true reasons. "I stumbled across a bit of information that may help me to achieve my goal."

"I don't understand. Did you find a way to inherit it early?"

Lilliana got up, walked to the window of the sitting room, and pulled open the curtains. She stared out at the garden and pondered how to explain what she overheard, and exactly how it fit into her idea to get everything she wanted. Various shades of roses, red, orange, and white, scattered across the garden in a pattern that reminded Lilliana of a kaleidoscope. The garden remained one of the places that she turned to when she needed to reflect on what floated through her mind. It calmed her and made it possible for her to think rationally about any issue that arose in her life. Something about being surrounded by the plant life helped her to think and form her plans with a clear head. Lilliana needed to get Gemma to aid her in her quest to leave England. They worked their magic on her as she calmly let the curtain go and turned back towards her best friend.

"I don't *ever* plan on getting married. I told you that the day we met. My parents still insisted on a season or two. They believe everyone is capable of finding love. They don't understand they are a rarity."

A sting of pain stabbed through her heart, Lilliana rubbed her chest in an attempt to erase the phantom ache. After her disastrous first season, she knew quite well how unusual it was for a love match to exist within the ton. Her choices were lecherous old men and scheming vermin only after her money. There was one man though who made her want to believe he really loved her. She found out the hard way he only wanted to use her. She was thankful he didn't achieve his goal and Lilliana came out relatively unscathed, but the damage to her belief in love sat firmly in place.

"Most matches are made for business or political

reasons. It's all about money and there is no way I'm handing over mine to a male to control."

Gemma tilted her head and crinkled her nose in confusion. Lilliana knew she didn't get it. Her friend wanted to get married and have children. The two years difference in their ages showed when they discussed the possibility of matrimony. In time, Lilliana believed Gemma would look back on this conversation with clarity. In the midst of starting her first season and barely seventeen years old, Gemma still approached life with rose-colored glasses on. For a brief moment in time Lilliana had worn that same veil of hope; her parent's love inspired her enough to want to find it herself.

Reality came crashing in like a bolt of lightning and shattered every ounce of optimism she held within her. Lilliana realized finding love at the various parties hosted within London society equaled finding a mythical creature. The chances of finding a unicorn would be an easier feat. So she gave up on love and formed a new plan for her life.

"I still think you are being preposterous. Why are you so against marriage?" Gemma folded her arms across her chest and stared at Lilliana. Her eyes pinning her in place as she spoke. "That's what a lady is expected to do after all. I just don't understand how you plan on claiming your inheritance without the benefit of a husband to help you get it."

Lilliana could feel her lips twitch into a smile. Her mother often commented on how Lilliana received all her father's traits, even his less than desirable ones. William Thorston Marsden, fifth Viscount Torrington, had a way of getting what he wanted out of people. She admired that characteristic in her father and sought to emulate it. Still, she wished she had been lucky enough to get her mother's pale blonde hair instead of her father's dark curls. In Lilliana's mind, her twin brother, Liam, was blessed because he inherited her mother's coloring.

"I suppose I should explain it so you won't be left in the dark. I'll need your assistance after all."

Gemma got up from her seat and crossed to the window where Lilliana still stood. "You're my best friend. I'll help if I can, but I'm going to be honest and say I don't like this. I don't want to lose you. Please reconsider."

"I will miss you, but I need to find my own way. Please understand this is the best thing for me."

Gemma sighed and then pulled Lilliana into her arms for a hug. Lilliana wrapped her arms around her best friend. She had been curious about Gemma once she realized who she was. Lady Gemma

Kemsley had been the girl her father wanted her brother to marry when they were younger. She sought out an introduction to get her measure and hadn't been disappointed in the young woman. They had only been friends for a few months, but in all her nineteen years she had never been close to another female her age. It didn't matter that a couple years separated their age; they were a different kind of soul mate. They appreciated each other on a level that no one else ever could or would.

"I'll try to understand. I really will, but I'm never going to like it. You are my only friend. I will always wish for you to be near me..." Gemma pulled away from Lilliana and clasped their hands together. "Tell me what I can do to help."

Lilliana knew she could count on Gemma. Elation filled her as she could envision how it would all work out. Now all she needed to do was give her all the details so she could do her part in the plan.

"I overheard my parents talking. I had no intention of listening until I heard my name spoken. I found out some interesting things that I never knew. Not the least being that Mama never intended to get married and Father had blackmailed her into agreeing to be his wife."

Gemma gasped. "What?"

"Makes you stop and question the validity of their love and all that doesn't it?"

Gemma's mouth hung open with shock radiating from her eyes. After a small pause while the information sank in she asked, "Why would he do such a thing?"

"Once upon a time Papa sailed his ship, the *Sea Rover*, as its pirate captain. Apparently he had a little feud with Mama's grandpere and she became the leverage he needed to enact his revenge. They came out of it okay, clearly as they are still together." Lilliana flipped her hand dismissively as she spoke. "The point is that Mama said that by the time I'm twenty if I still don't wish to wed, she planned on giving me the deed to the plantation in South Carolina."

Lilliana tried over and over to explain to her parents how much marriage was distasteful to her, without going into too much detail. If her father knew exactly how her heart had been bruised, he would have murderous intentions. The real issue was she didn't want anyone to know how naïve she had been. Now, she knew she could get what she wanted and nothing made her happier. Anxiety filled with equal swirls of excitement tumbled through her belly.

"That's still too long for me to wait. I won't be twenty until December and that is nine months away. What I want to do is sail there now and use my family position to gain control. My plans are not going to change just because nine months pass by."

"What good will that do? Without the deed securely in your control will they allow you to oversee the plantation? Isn't someone already there taking care of the property?" Gemma asked.

"There is an overseer yes. I'm hoping to convince him that the letter giving him orders to give me control got lost on the mail packet before my arrival. Come let's sit down in comfort as we work out the details." Lilliana grabbed Gemma's hand and led her to the settee. After they were seated she poured them both tea and handed a cup to her friend. Lilliana took a sip of tea before continuing their conversation. "I've thought a lot about what needs to be done. Even if the overseer doesn't believe I have control of the plantation no one has the authority to throw me off the property because it is owned by my family. If I have to wait, I'd rather do it in South Carolina."

Gemma nodded. "Okay, I suppose that makes sense. What do you need me to do?"

"Well the tricky part is leaving without letting my

parents know. First, I need to find a ship sailing to America. Once I book passage I'm going to need a way to get my trunks on board without raising suspicion. I'm not worried about funds. I've been saving all my pin money for months now." Lilliana gave Gemma a smile. Surely she would see how she thought of every possible issue in her plan.

"So how do you plan on getting your trunks on board the ship?"

"That is where you come in. Once I know what ship I'm on, I'd like you to invite me to come stay with you in the country for a week." Lilliana set her teacup down and gave Gemma her full attention. She really needed Gemma to help her. If she didn't, her whole plan would fall apart. Her eyes pleaded with Gemma as she spoke, "My family won't question it because they know that our schedule is relaxed at the moment. It will give me a reason to pack a trunk or two and have them loaded onto a carriage. The carriage with your family crest on it that is."

"Oh, I understand. You will have the carriage drop you off at the docks and our servants will unload your trunks to be delivered to the ship. They won't have a reason to let your family know that you're boarding the ship. The servants will assume they already know." Gemma nodded her head in understanding.

"I knew you'd get it." Excitement filled Lilliana's voice. "It's all coming together now. I only have one little facet to figure out before I can iron out the rest of the details. The first item I need to cross off my list is to figure out what ships are heading to America and if they are accepting passengers."

"However are you going to figure that out?"

"Oh, that's the easy part. I will just ask Liam," Lilliana proclaimed.

Gemma blinked several times before she asked, "Won't he find that suspicious?"

"Not at all," Lilliana said waving her hand. "He's constantly talking about the Marsden shipping line and its competitors. He just started to take over the business. Our father believes it's time for him to learn about his future inheritance."

"I see. When do you plan on getting the information out of him?"

"Tonight at the Silverton's ball. Father is making him escort me. I will make sure to have a friendly conversation with him in the carriage on our way."

"You have thought of everything. I'm sure it will work just the way you want it." A small smile grew on Gemma's face as she looked at Lilliana. "I just wish your plans didn't have to take you so far away from England. Why couldn't you have fallen in love with a nice earl or baron...or even a mere mister? Anything that might inspire you to stay where I have an actual possibility to visit you, chances are I'll never be able to travel to America to visit. Promise me you'll come back to see me."

"I promise to come back to see you. In the meantime, we'll keep in touch with lots and lots of letters. I want to know everything about your life and when you find the man of your dreams."

"Good. I suppose I should go. I'll see you tonight at the ball."

Gemma stood up and grabbed her pelisse. After she donned it, she walked over and gave Lilliana a quick hug. She watched as Gemma left the room and got up to walk back to the window to look at the rose garden. All she could do at this point was hope all of her plans went off without a hitch. Doubts clouded her mind as she knew from experience nothing ever went exactly as planned, and naught could be done to alleviate her anxiety. Lilliana decided to try and let it go. She turned and left the sitting room to find some kind of diversion. Perhaps a book would work to distract her thoughts away from any possible problems—thinking, or over thinking in her case, had always been her worst enemy. With a smile on her lips Lilliana strolled to the library. Dark feelings would not sink through and ruin her good mood. Preparation was the key to success. No one planned and schemed better than Lilliana Marsden.

Order Here

EXCERPT: A SANGUINE GEM

A MARSDEN ROMANCE BOOK THREE

DAWN BROWER

USA TODAY
BESTSELLING AUTHOR

Dawn
Brower

A MARSDEN
ROMANCE

A
Sanguine
Gem

CHAPTER ONE

*L*iam Marsden had a lot of things on his mind. However, he couldn't dwell on what was beyond his control. He had more pressing issues to deal with, starting with a meeting his father demanded. He had never let him down before, and he had no intention of starting at this juncture of his life.

He walked into his family home and strolled down the hallway towards the study. As he opened the door, he got a brief look at his father engrossed in his own work. The viscount had his dark hair pulled back at the nape of his neck; loose strands fell over his forehead as he tilted his head to read the paper in front of him. Liam had always admired his tenacity and willingness to do anything to accomplish any task. He didn't give up easily and believed the world belonged to him to take what he wanted from it.

"Ah good you're here," He glanced up at Liam and set his work aside. "I have a few things I need to discuss with you."

"I came as soon as I received your missive. What's so urgent?"

"A good number of things that I didn't foresee."

On closer scrutiny, Liam could see stress lines forming on his father's face. His eyes filled with worry as he rubbed his temples. What could have happened to make him appear so concerned? Liam didn't think this meeting would be a jovial one. His father didn't often worry about things. No, Viscount Torrington took action and left the fretting to others.

"This is serious?" Liam asked as he raised an eyebrow.

"I received a letter from your sister. Some of it is good news. Most of it is actually."

"It's the part that isn't good news that concerns you." Liam sat down and leaned forward, giving his father his full attention. "What has happened?"

"First, I should tell you that you are the proud uncle of a strapping baby boy. You sister had her child a month ago. They named him William Jamieson after his two grandfathers. Poor boy has a lot to live up to with that name." He laughed.

"If I'm an uncle that means you are a grandfather. How does that make you feel old man" Liam grinned. He couldn't resist an opportunity to tease his father.

"Bite your tongue, boy. It'll be a long time before I'm an old man," With a devilish grin on his face, his father sat back in his chair and studied Liam. "This is good for you because I don't think you are quite ready to fill my shoes."

Liam hoped his father lived a very long life. He couldn't imagine a life without the man's robust personality filling a room wherever he went. Like most children, he believed his parents infallible. He knew they were mere human beings, but he liked to believe they would live forever.

"No, I can't say I'm in a hurry to take the reins from you. I pray you're here for many years to come. For more reasons than one," Liam said. "But regardless of how I feel about your possible demise that isn't why you summoned me here. Nor is it the news about my new nephew. Grateful as I am to hear about it, something else weighs on your mind. I think it's time to dispense with the pleasantries."

"That isn't all your sister wrote about," he said with a heavy sigh. "She has some concerns that she asked me to look into."

"Is it about the merger of Marsden Shipping with RandCo? There isn't an issue with its completion, is there?" He needed to dispense with that bit of concern first because it was at the forefront of his mind. "If so, I'd like to take care of it immediately."

"No, that at least is going well. We should have considered a merger as soon as Lily and Rand married." Viscount Torrington sighed and stood up. He strolled over to a nearby shelf and pulled out a decanter of brandy along with two glasses. "This is something entirely different and I'm not sure how to proceed."

"What's Lily worried about?" Liam's concern rose. What could be so dreadful?

Viscount Torrington handed Liam a brandy filled snifter. He took a sip of his own and set it down. He stared past Liam, his eyes unfocused. "The Earl of Devon was a pretty good friend of mine."

"I remember." Liam nodded.

"At one time I'd hope to have a merger with him," his father paused and stared down at his drink. "It was the reason we attempted to betroth you and Gemma."

Liam would rather forget about that time in his life. He grimaced and stared up at his father. "Right, that was several years ago." What was his father getting at?

"The business merger and familial one fell through at the same time. We never found a reason to revisit either." He downed the rest of his drink in his glass. "I have to admit a part of me is glad it didn't. As much as I liked the man I abhor the gentleman who inherited his estate."

Liam rubbed his temple; a pain throbbed through his head listening to his father rattle on. "What does Alfie have to do with this?"

"Lady Gemma is my concern."

She wasn't his, so Liam had no clue why he brought her into the conversation. In fact, everything he'd said so far hadn't made any sense to him.

"Father, what exactly is the problem?" Frustration built to the boiling point deep inside him. "I don't understand what Lady Gemma has to do with all of this."

"Lady Gemma keeps in touch with Lily. She wrote your sister about some disturbing news."The viscount sat back and studied Liam. He steepled his hands together as he spoke. "She thinks I might have a solution to the problem. I can think of a couple of ways we could assist her, but you would have to be willing."

"What it is you would like me to do?" Liam replied, a horrible feeling sinking to the bottom of his gut.

Viscount Torrington leaned forward and set his hands on his desk. His eyes bore into Liam's as he appeared to weigh over the issue that troubled him.

"You know I'd never force you to do anything, but I think in this you believe as I do."

"I'm at a loss as you haven't explained anything to me," Liam reminded him. "How am I to know if I agree or not if you don't?" He silently hoped his father wasn't about to ask what he thought he was. After he mentioned the botched attempt to betroth him to Lady Gemma, Liam couldn't help but wonder —he couldn't possibly want him to marry Gemma. *Could he?*

"First, you should be aware of the circumstances regarding Lady Gemma and why Lily is so concerned," his father told him. "Then I will explain my idea and the two possible solutions to it. One is a better option, and the other should only be considered if you are against the first."

"And what is happening with her?" Liam stood up and paced around the room. He stopped a few steps away and pinned his father with a stare. "Quit stalling and tell me what's going on."

"Alfie is—being difficult."

"In what way?"

If his father didn't tell him what was going on soon. Liam wouldn't be held responsible for his actions. Their conversation was driving him mad.

"He has squandered the entire inheritance. If the estate weren't entailed, he'd sell it to pay off his enormous debts. That leaves him in a bit of a bind. He needs money and as fast as possible."

Liam nodded. "I think I see the correlation. Lady Gemma still has an inheritance, and he wants to get his hands on it."

Viscount Torrington stood up and joined him in front of the desk. His eyes had an angry edge to them. Liam knew his father well enough to realize he wanted to do some damage to the new Earl of Devon. Whatever Alfie was doing enraged him. Liam had a bad feeling about what was going on with Lily's friend.

"In a manner of speaking yes and he is willing to use whatever is at his disposal to get it. Lady Gemma is afraid he might force the situation to get his way."

"I see." Liam scowled. "Does she have reason to believe he will act so dishonorably?"

"This is old news." His father frowned and crossed his arms over his chest. "I got the letter today from your sister. It might already be a foregone conclusion. I'm afraid we may be too late with how slow mail travels between England and America. I don't know what we'll find if we go to the Earl of Devon's estate."

Not good news, in fact, they were quite horrid. Liam might have issues with Lady Gemma, but he'd never wanted anyone to hurt her. He'd willingly help her deal with her cousin if he could find a good solution to her problem.

"I hadn't even considered that. We are wasting time. What are your solutions?" Liam asked.

"Lady Gemma needs a husband. She doesn't gain majority and control over her funds for five more years. She only has one solution that will effectively work for her."

With those words, Liam's fears were realized. His heart beat faster in his chest and the pounding in his head intensified.

His father wanted him to marry Lady Gemma.

Liam should be appalled at the suggestion, especially as he'd already tried to betroth them when they were younger. He had never denied that Lady Gemma had beauty in spades. She had luxurious crimson hair and eyes the color of jade. His mouth watered thinking about her beautiful complexion and soft curves. That was until she open her mouth to speak. Listening to her droll on and on for what seemed like forever, he invariably forgot how exquisite her body and face appeared and wanted to put some much needed distance between them.

Why should he sacrifice his life for her?

The brazen redhead had been the bane of his existence for several years now. It took the death of her father for her to back away. Admittedly he admired her tenacity and willingness to make her wishes known, but that didn't mean he ever desired to tie himself to her forever. Perhaps his father's other solution would be easier for him to stomach.

"You are not suggesting what I think you are." Appalled, Liam sat back down in his chair. Shock filled him to the brink. He had to be reading the situation wrong.

"I had hoped that you had some tender feelings for the chit. You are constantly arguing with her." His father sat back down in his chair, a slight knowing smirk resting on his face. "That is a form of passion. Trust me I know a bit about denial in that area."

"Well, you're incorrect in your assumption." Liam

glared. He didn't have any feelings for Gemma. She was a nuisance nothing more. "There aren't any tender feelings on either side. The girl irritates me to no end. I never did understand what Lily saw in her."

"That's too bad. I still have the betrothal contract I signed with Lady Gemma's father. We could have used it to our advantage."

Liam stared at his father with a blank expression. He'd actually signed the contract? How could he have done that? His father had reassured him he'd never force him to marry anyone.

"Excuse me could you repeat that? I don't think I heard you correctly." Liam hoped he'd heard wrong. Sadly he doubted he had. "You informed me the betrothal hadn't been finalized."

"That's correct," His father grinned. "However Devon hoped I'd change my mind and told me to keep the contract. All I have to do to make it legal is sign my name to it."

Liam blanched. His father was losing his mind. There wasn't a chance in hell he'd make him marry Lady Gemma. "But you're not going to, right

"So you are not willing to help?"

"I didn't say that." Liam shook his head. "I'm willing to hear the other plan you have. I'm hoping it is preferable to the latter."

"The other plan involves you basically kidnapping the girl and taking her to your sister in South Carolina."

Relief flooded him at his father's words. Calm now that the storm of anxiety fled his stomach, Liam took a deep breath and considered his father's other idea. He had to agree that the second plan held more appeal. It was preferable, but not that much better in the grand scheme of things. He would still be forced to spend a considerable amount of time in Lady Gemma's company. How would he be able to get through a voyage with her? They would have to take the Sea Rover for the crossing. No other ships were available, and their steamships were only in the planning stages of being built. If he had any luck, it wouldn't take more than three weeks to complete.

The bonus, of course, would be to see his sister and his new nephew. He sincerely wished to see them so that no price was too high for him to be able to spend time in their company. He would even be willing to get to know his brother-in-law as well. Maybe he would find a way to like the rat bastard. His father may have forgiven him for stealing Lily, but Liam didn't feel like he deserved such absolution. The man had a lot of audacity to run away with the daughter of Viscount Torrington—a former pirate. Liam would give him that much.

"That plan is more conceivable to accomplish," Liam said. "But is kidnapping really necessary? Do you believe Lady Gemma will be unwilling to go to live with Lily?"

"I honestly do not know," his father sighed. "I hate to tell you this, but I think you're going to need ammunition to get her out."

"Explain," Liam demanded.

"If you go in prepared Alfie won't have anything to argue about."

"How do you suggest I do that?"

His father grinned. It almost had a wicked tinge to it. "I'm going to sign this betrothal. Go to the bishop and demand a special license. With the right amount of money and the betrothal as evidence, he won't deny you."

"I fail to see why I need to go to such lengths."

"Alfie won't let Gemma go willingly. You're going to have to force his hand." His father paused and looked him in the eye. "I'm not telling you to marry the girl. Just use the tools I'm giving you to save her."

"All right I will go see the bishop now. Afterward, I will retrieve Gemma and bring her back here to plan our next move." Liam said.

"Good. I'd hate to disappoint your sister. I hope we are not too late to help Lady Gemma."

With those words, Liam got up and walked out of the study. He had never been a fan of Lady Gemma Kemsley, but he had never wished her ill will either. If she had more trouble than she could handle, Liam had no choice but to help her. His sister depended on him, and he had never let her down before—he certainly didn't plan on starting with Lady Gemma.

The chit had better be prepared to do everything necessary to leave her home. Liam didn't suffer fools and luckily for him he knew that she didn't either. No matter what he believed, her to be he had always been able to see the keen intelligence in her eyes. Perhaps with age she had also gained some maturity to go along with it.

Order Here

www.ingramcontent.com/pod-product-compliance
Lightning Source LLC
Chambersburg PA
CBHW030636130626
46552CB00002B/874